BOUGHT BY HER BOSS

KAYLEE MONROE

BOUGHT BY HER BOSS

The only thing being a "good girl" has gotten me was the ability to auction off my v-card to help my sister in rehab. Now, I'm ready to be a bad girl for the highest bidder.

Imagine my shock and excitement when it's my older, sexy boss who wins me for the night, until Donovan insists he didn't buy my v-card to take it, which is disappointing to say the least. He only meant to protect me from any other man who might take advantage of me.

What I want is Donovan to take advantage of me, anyway he likes, even knowing he has a dominant side. And when he drops his guard just enough for me to realize that my feelings are not one-sided, that's when I decide to turn the tables and seduce him . . . until he makes it very clear that he's going to be the one in charge and the term "boss" takes on a whole other meaning.

CHAPTER 1

Jessica

There were days when I felt trapped in my life. This morning was one of those times. I stared down at the letter wondering how I was going to pay the amount owed. It wasn't a huge amount. It wasn't even an unreasonable one, but on my budget it might as well have been a million bucks.

I was already a month behind on rent and the utilities all seemed to be coming in at the same time. If I was being honest I'd admit I needed help, but there was no one to offer a hand. I was on my own and I didn't really understand how completely alone I was until this moment.

I stuffed the letter in my purse, forcing my tears not to fall and slipped my feet into my pumps. The obvious answer was for Krissy to get a job and help pay her way, but my sister hadn't managed to keep a single job for more than a week in her entire life.

Thinking about Krissy made my eyes slide in the direction of her room.

I hadn't seen her for a week, which wasn't unusual for Krissy. She disappeared all the time. She'd show up eventually, dirty and needing a good meal, usually coming down from whatever high she was on. No matter how many times I begged her to calm down and take things easy she never did. I was worried the drugs were going to kill her.

My sister took the whole good and bad twin thing a little too seriously.

Krissy had always been wild. Even growing up she had pushed every single boundary our parents put in place. She would never do as she was told, so I didn't know why I expected her to change now.

These past few years though her behavior had moved from wild to downright dangerous. I was scared for my twin. She had a reckless streak that made me fear one day she'd go too far and I'd lose her.

That was part of the reason why our parents cut her off.

They were tired of watching her self-destruct.

I understood it. I really did. I loved Krissy more than anyone, but it was hard to watch someone you love throw their life away. Krissy excelled at that, but I could never turn my back on her.

I don't know how our parents could.

They hated who she was. She embarrassed them and no matter how many times she was punished Krissy never changed or amended her behavior.

In many ways, I admired her for standing up to them, for pushing the crazy boundaries they put in place. I never could. I was the good girl. The twenty-three year old virgin. I never put a foot wrong forward, but despite that I was still punished for Krissy's messes.

Even so, I chose to stick by my sister. She was my twin and I couldn't walk away, even if I wanted to. As a result my parents severed all ties with me too.

Sometimes, I wondered if I really knew what I was getting into when I sided with her. Keeping my sister out of trouble was a full time job—one that didn't pay.

I didn't regret my choice. It was crazy to say that considering the shit she put me through, but it wasn't her fault.

She had a disease. The worst one.

Addiction was no joke.

I glanced down at my watch. I was going to be late for the job that did keep a roof over our heads.

I grabbed my keys off the kitchen counter and rushed for the door.

During the bus ride to work, I found myself scrolling job ads on my phone. I worked full time in an office, but I could maybe fit in a second job at a bar in the evening.

Who needed sleep, right?

It would take some pressure off and maybe help shift some of the mounting bills.

By the time I reached the stop near the office, I was already tired. This was going to be a long day.

I headed into the building and used the elevator to get to the floor I worked on. My office was bright, modern, and classy. I'd been working here for more than a year as assistant to the CEO. I loved my job—and my gorgeous, hot boss made my days a little brighter.

I placed my purse on my desk and popped my head around Mr. Black's door. His office was empty. I made it in before him, which was always a good thing. I didn't like it if he needed me and I wasn't here.

I moved back to my desk and loaded up my computer. There was a stack of messages waiting to be dealt with and I needed to organize Mr. Black's diary for the day, making sure he had all the documents and notes he needed for his meetings. It was a routine I was more than used to and I did it on autopilot.

My cell phone buzzed on the desk next to me.

I wasn't supposed to take personal calls at work, but the number on the screen was not one I recognized despite being local. Knowing what my sister was like, I found my finger swiping over the screen before I realized what I was doing.

"Hello?"

There was a long sigh in my ear. "I'm sorry," Krissy mumbled.

"Where are you?" I demanded, twisting slightly so I wouldn't be overheard by anyone on my floor. "I've been worried."

"I was in the hospital."

A tingle of fear went through me. "Are you all right?"

"I overdosed," she said groggily. "Now they're forcing me into some shitty rehab center. I won't go."

I closed my eyes, trying to steady my breath, which felt lodged in my chest. My fear for my sister grew like a poison spreading through my veins. "Where are you now?"

"About to be transferred."

"What happened?"

"It was an accident. I didn't mean for it to happen, but the doc's think I'm a risk to myself. They're forcing me into rehab. I don't need it. It's fucking stupid."

She was in denial. She needed help and had done so for a long time. I'd tried so many times over the years to get her into a facility but she'd never stay more than a few hours. If I could get her to stay this time it might just be enough to crack this addiction and get my sister back on the road to recovery.

It might be enough to get my sister back, period.

"You OD'd. You need to be there, Krissy." My words are pointed.

"You got the money to pay for this shit? Because it's expensive as hell. I mean, they've brought me here against my will and they expect me to pay for the privilege."

My stomach churned. How the hell was I going to pay for rehab as well as everything else? "I'll sort the payment out," I assured her, wondering even as I said it how I was going to make that happen. "I just want you to get better."

"There's nothing wrong with me," she insisted.

"Krissy, I know you don't want to hear it, but you're sick. This addiction will eat you alive if you don't get help. I can't lose you. Please, do this for both of us. I need you."

She went quiet for a moment. "You're asking a lot, Jessica."

"I'm asking for you to fight," I said, a knot of emotion in my throat. "I can't lose my other half."

My voice was laced with pain and I felt it deep in my gut. Movement caught my attention and I glanced up from the desk to see that my boss, Donovan Black, had arrived. I got momentarily distracted by him, a daily occurrence whenever he was in my sphere.

The man was sex on legs. Tall, handsome, with dark blond hair and a hint of scruff covering a strong jawline. He always wore tailored suits that fit him perfectly and today was no different. The crisp white shirt he was wearing was unbuttoned at the neck, showing a tantalizing hint of his chest. My thoughts verged on inappropriate as I took him in. It was a sin to look as good as he did.

He raised a brow at me before he disappeared into his office.

"Krissy, I've got to go," I said in a rush. "Stay in the rehab center. I'll take care of the payment."

Somehow.

I hung up on my sister and took a deep breath. The weight of everything was starting to feel like it was crushing my shoulders. How much more pressure could I honestly take before I broke completely?

I thought about the outstanding bill stuffed in my purse and tried not to cry.

It was starting to feel like I had no way out of this mess.

Taking a deep breath, I pushed my emotions down and walked into Mr. Black's office. He was shrugging out of his suit jacket as I entered and I took a moment to admire the strong muscles of his back before he turned to me. I snapped my eyes to his face, forcing a smile on my face.

"Morning," I said, keeping my tone light, even though I felt anything but.

"Who is your 'other half'?" he ask, without muttering so much as a greeting back.

I frowned, wondering just how much of the conversation he heard. "That would be my twin sister, Krissy."

His brows lifted up his forehead. "I didn't know you had a twin." I didn't talk about my personal life, so I'm not surprised about that. "Should I be scared there are two of you?"

He smiled as he said it and butterflies filled my stomach. I shouldn't be lusting over my boss. I'm sure there was a special seat reserved in hell for assistants who did.

"Believe me, we're nothing alike." I handed him his schedule. "You have a meeting in twenty minutes with the head of finance and HR wants to talk to you whenever you have a free moment."

He grumbled about the latter. He hated dealing with HR and all the red tape they insisted on.

I left his office and returned to my computer. For the next hour I scrolled through reports and the tasks I had to complete. I was just starting to get into my stride when my phone vibrated on the desk next to me.

Glancing around, I saw I was alone and

Mr. Black's door was closed so I ducked out into the corridor and I answered the phone.

"Hello?" I said quietly.

"Hi, is this Jessica Bennett?

"Yes." My stomach twisted. The caller sounded official and official callers usually wanted money from me.

"This is Myra from the billing department at St Augustine's Hospital." My stomach sank. I didn't expect the hospital to get in touch so soon. "You're listed as the next of kin for Krissy Bennett."

Of course I was.

"I need to discuss payment for the hospital stay and the rehab center she's a patient at."

She rattled off a figure that made my entire body jolt. There were a lot of zeros in the amount she gave me. More zeros than I could pay on my currently salary, or even if I took on another job.

"Will that be okay? We can arrange a payment schedule as soon as you confirm."

No, it's not okay. I bit my bottom lip, trying to work out where this money was going to come from. "Yes. It'll be fine."

"Great! Have a good day."

She hung up and I resisted the urge to sag against the wall. My phone started buzzing almost immediately. With trepidation I glanced down at the screen and saw it was my best friend, Kyra.

I answered it. "Hey."

"Where've you been, stranger?"

I winced. I've been a little distance and my hectic schedule meant I'd ducked out on meeting her the last few times.

"Sorry."

"Don't be sorry, just meet me for lunch."

I really didn't feel like putting on a front, even though Kyra wouldn't expect me to, but she had no idea how bad things were for me. "I don't know…"

"Girl, I haven't seen you in forever. Don't make me come down to your office and drag you out of it."

I snorted, because she would do it. "Fine. I get off in thirty minutes. Meet me in the usual place."

I finished up what I needed to and then grabbed my purse and jacket. Mr. Black was still in his meeting and would be for a while longer, but I ordered food for him before I left.

As soon as I stepped foot inside the restaurant, I saw Kyra sitting in a booth. She looked amazing. Her hair was perfect, her makeup pristine and her clothes looked expensive. Kyra never hurt for money before. She came from a well off family and she had a decent job, but the jewelry, designer clothes and accessories she wore reeked of wealth.

"You look out of this world," I told her with a smile.

"Being an accountant pays well."

My brows raised. "Maybe I should change jobs. I'm clearly in the wrong career."

"Hey, if you ever want to change occupations I'll help you get started. It's very lucrative."

I took a seat opposite her. She'd already ordered me a coffee so I lifted the mug and took a sip.

"I'm not good with numbers," I told her truthfully. "Isn't that kind of important for accountants?"

"What about penises?"

I nearly sprayed my coffee over the table

at that odd comment. She smiled at me, her eyes filled with mischief, but she was serious.

"I don't know. I've never tried one," I admitted.

Kyra raised a brow as she wrapped her hands around her own mug. "I didn't have you pegged as a taco lover."

"Tacos? Who doesn't love tacos?"

She laughed, and I felt like I wasn't on the same page as her. "I don't really mean tacos. I mean… hoo-hahs."

I gave her a blank look. I had no idea what she was talking about.

She leaned forward and said, "Vaginas."

I was sure my face was on fire. It wasn't unusual for Kyra to talk like this, but for some reason it always embarrassed me. Maybe it was my lack of experience.

"I can't believe you just said that," I hissed at her, glancing around to make sure we weren't overheard." She leaned back in her seat, grinning. "And no. I'm just… a virgin. Okay?"

She didn't judge me for that, which I was grateful for. I already felt embarrassed that I was still carrying around my v-card. Most people my age were sexually active.

"The offer still stands. You'd make an excellent accountant."

I wasn't entirely sure what we were talking about and what kind of accountancy she did, but I got the feeling it didn't really include numbers.

"Thanks for the offer. I'll think about it."

She grinned. "Think carefully."

CHAPTER 2

Donovan

essica was late back from lunch. It didn't bother me—she was such a good assistant I would forgive the minor infraction—but I was worried about her. For the past few weeks she had been... different.

Sad.

I don't know how else to describe her demeanor, but that covered it.

I didn't like that she seemed so unhappy, and I didn't like that I didn't know why either. Jessica wasn't the kind of woman to discuss her problems, and especially not with me, but I got the impression she was in some kind of difficulty. I wished she would open up so I could help her.

I sipped my coffee, trying to work out what was going on in my pretty little assistant's life.

She'd been working with me for a while now and if I was being honest I'd admit she was the best assistant I'd ever had. She knew what I needed without me having to tell her sometimes, as if she was in my brain. That intuition made us a perfect fit.

But she wasn't happy.

Was it the job?

Was it me?

Was I overbearing? Too demanding?

I didn't think it was me, but something was certainly wrong.

Thinking about Jessica was dangerous. As soon as her image flashed in my mind, my cock started to swell in my pants. She always had that effect on me. She was delectable. Innocent, beautiful, smart, and the way she looked in that tight pencil skirt yesterday…

My mouth watered just thinking about it. She had a gorgeous figure, great tits too. She'd leaned over the desk to reach for a pen from my drawer and I nearly came undone. It had distracted me enough from my conversation on the phone that I'd had to hang up so I could give her my full attention.

My desire for her was inappropriate.

She was an employee, but I couldn't stop from lusting after her. It didn't matter that there was over a decade between us. It didn't matter that I'd been considering leaving the company and selling the business before she became my assistant. She was the reason I was still here. She'd helped me to find a renewed passion for my work.

Nothing could happen between us. I was too old for her. Most of the time I pretended I was protective of her, like a big brother would be, but the truth was she made my heart stutter in my chest when she was in my presence.

When I'd heard her mention her other half when on the phone my fists had curled into balls. Had I let her slip through my fingers? Had I allowed another man to claim what should have been mine?

The jealousy that rose inside me was both surprising and a little alarming. I wasn't used to wanting women I couldn't have. I was the kind of man who took what he wanted.

And what I wanted was her.

I'd been unable to stop my question from coming out harsh. I didn't want to lose her to someone else—even though I didn't plan to claim her either, which made me a grade A dick.

I didn't expect her to tell me she had a sister.

She'd never mentioned a twin before. Thinking about it, Jessica never talked about her family at all. I had no idea if she was close with her parents, if she had an abundance of friends. What she did after she was done at the office.

For some reason, I now wanted to know.

I glanced down at my watch. It was 2:15pm. She was really late back from lunch and I was starting to get worried.

Just as I was considering calling her cell, she hurried up the corridor, looking frazzled.

I moved to the doorway of my office, leaning against the jamb.

"I'm so sorry I'm late, Mr. Black."

She tossed her purse on her desk and shrugged out of her jacket. "It's fine," I told her. "Are you all right?"

The smile Jessica gave me was forced. "The traffic was awful getting back from lunch."

I took another sip of my coffee, even though it was tepid. I needed something to do with my hands because she was bending over the desk to stash her purse in her cabinet at the side of the desk. It gave me an eye full of her breasts. The gentlemanly thing to do would have been to look away. But I'd never been a gentleman.

"Did you have fun at lunch?" I asked, glancing away when she straightened. I didn't want to get caught ogling her.

"I did. Mostly. There's photo evidence of just how much fun on Instagram." She brushed her fingers through her hair and then smiled at me. "I'll have the notes you need for your three pm meeting ready in ten minutes."

I nodded. "Thanks."

I headed into my office, leaving the door open and sat in front of my computer. For a few moments I pulled up my emails and responded to a few, but then my mind drifted back to Jessica. Her mention of Instagram intrigued me.

Before I could even contemplate how many lines I was crossing, I pulled up Instagram and searched her name. There were a few accounts that came up, but I recognized her image. I clicked on her face and her page loaded.

There were tons of photos, but I focused on the most recent.

She was with a tiny brunette in most of them, smiling, but I noticed her smile didn't quite reach her eyes.

The brunette caught my attention. She looked familiar. The caption said, 'Lunch with Kyra.'

Kyra…

Who was she?

The more I looked at her, the more certain I was that I knew her. "Where does Kyra work?" I muttered to myself.

"I don't know."

I jumped nearly out of my seat, peering over the top of my monitor. Jessica was standing in front of my desk. I was glad she couldn't see my screen and how much of a stalker I was being.

"She said she's an accountant," Jessica said.

The little wrinkle between her brows when she said that was adorable.

I glanced back at the picture.

An accountant?

Then it clicked. I smirked. Is that what they were calling themselves? Accountants? I doubted Kyra had ever seen a single spreadsheet in her life. Kyra worked at a very exclusive club. That was where I recognized her from. It was a club that catered to a specific clientele—one that indulged in sex.

Kyra was a sex worker.

I clicked out of the window, closing Instagram and losing Jessica's image.

"Do you know her?" she asked, tipping her head curiously.

"No," I said softly, noticing the slight hint of jealousy in her tone. I liked that it was there, but I wasn't sure if she realized how she'd sounded. "I've seen her around, but we've never spoken."

Her cell phone started to ring in the outer office, and she winced. "I'm sorry. I know I'm supposed to limit personal calls at work, but I need to take that call."

"By all means."

I wanted to tell her if she needed help I was here for her, but I said nothing. I just watched through the window that over-looked her desk as she returned to her seat, her phone pressed to her ear. I couldn't hear what she was saying, but I could see the tightness in her shoulders.

The phone on my desk started to ring. There were only a few people who had my direct number, so I picked it up instantly.

"Donovan Black."

"Hey, bud, how's it going?"

I grinned at the voice on the other end of the line. Archer and I had been friends for years. I met him in college and he was the one who introduced me to a world I didn't know existed, but one I very much enjoyed.

"You know—same shit, different day." I glanced up through the window and saw

Jessica was no longer at her desk. I resisted the urge to hang up on Archer to go and find her.

"Then I've got just the thing you need," Archer said. "Let off some steam at the club tonight."

The best way to get over someone was getting under someone else, but for some reason that didn't hold any appeal. "Can't tonight," I lied.

"You don't know what you're missing."

I did, and that was the problem. I wanted someone unattainable. I wanted Jessica.

"At least come on Friday if you won't come tonight. It's going to be an amusing evening."

My interest was piqued. "Why is that?"

"It's a themed night," he reminded me.

The club ran a themed night once a month and they were usually a good time.

"Out of curiosity, what's the theme this time?" I asked.

"Virgins." Archer chuckled.

I groaned. "Oh hell."

"Yeah, so be there and I'm not taking no

for an answer. If anything, it'll be fun to watch."

"Fine, I'll go," I promised, deciding I could use the distraction.

"Later, Donovan."

I hung up, wondering what the hell I'd got myself into.

CHAPTER 3

Jessica

I stared at the latest invoice from Krissy's rehab treatment. The amount made my eyes water and my gut clench. I needed to call to make a payment, but in truth I wasn't sure where that money was coming from. I'd spent everything I had from my own paycheck this month and I'd maxed out my credit card to pay for her first week there.

Now, they needed more money and I wasn't sure how the hell I was going to get it.

I didn't want to pull Krissy out of the facility. That was not an option. The treatment was working—or it seemed to be. It was early yet, and it would take time for her to get clean, but already I could see a difference in my sister during my visit yesterday evening.

She was more settled. More like the Krissy I remembered before the drugs got a stranglehold on her. Before addiction consumed her life. I wanted her to prove our parents wrong. I wanted her to make something of herself. I wasn't ready to give up on my sister.

I didn't think I ever would be.

But the center was pricey and bills were stacking up. I was already struggling to pay the everyday utilities and rent. This was wiping me out faster than I could raise what I needed to.

I'd tried to re-negotiate a payment schedule, but the billing department could only reduce my payments by a hundred dollars a month. It was something, but it wasn't enough.

My debts were growing faster than I could pay them back.

I needed money. Now.

If I couldn't pay the center they would kick her out and she'd go right back to her old habits. I was truly worried the next time she overdosed could be the last time. She was already walking a tightrope with her life. She'd had more second chances than I could count. It was only a matter of time before her luck ran out.

She needed the treatment, as expensive as it was.

I'd been trying to find a second job for extra income, but I'd heard nothing. I'd applied to bars, even a security job. I didn't hear back from any of them.

Staring at the bill made my stomach twist. I was out of options—and time.

Desperation had me grabbing my phone and pulling up Kyra's contact details. I paused for a moment before hitting the call button. I didn't want Kyra to know I was struggling, but I needed this.

She was my only chance.

She picked up on the third ring.

"Hey, girl. How are you?" The happiness in her voice made me smile.

"I'm good." That was a lie, but I'd gotten so used to perpetuating it. I bit my bottom lip and then decided the only way to do this was to rip off the Band Aid. "I think I might need to take you up on your offer."

"Which offer?"

"The job."

"Is everything okay?"

I wanted to tell her what was going on with my sister. I wanted someone to tell me things would be all right, but I didn't want her to feel sorry for me either. This mess was mine to clean up, not Kyra's. If she could get me the job and it paid decently, I might just about be able to keep my head above the water threatening to drown me.

"I just need the money. Is there some kind of training? I'll do whatever you need." I winced internally as I asked, "Is there any way I can work as an accountant at night? I need to keep my day job."

There was silence for a moment before she said, "I only work at night."

This confused me. What kind of accountant worked nights only? It was good for me, because I could fit it around my schedule, but I still found myself saying, "But you're an accountant…"

Kyra made a funny noise. "I'm not really an accountant, Jessica."

I didn't understand what she was saying. "So there's no accounting job?"

"Oh there's a job. It just doesn't involve looking at figures and spreadsheets."

I rubbed at my forehead in confusion. "I'm lost."

"I just tell people I'm an accountant to hide what I really do."

"And what do you really do?"

"Are you sure you want to know?"

I wasn't sure about anything right now, but I nodded. "Yes, tell me."

"I work in a sex club. I'm a sex worker."

She couldn't have shocked me more if she'd tried. I didn't speak. I wasn't sure I trusted myself to respond. She was a sex worker? What did that mean? What did she do?

My thoughts collided in a messy jumble that I couldn't sort through. How did I never know this about Kyra? She was my best friend. How did she even get into this?

"You're a what?" I practically squealed.

"A sex worker." Before I could even contemplate what that meant, she continued to speak. "It's really a good job. The pay is amazing and it's exciting. Plus who doesn't enjoy sex?"

Considering I'd never tried it I wasn't sure what the fuss was about. I blinked frantically as I tried to compute the fact that my best friend sold her body for money.

"You're serious?"

"As a heart attack."

"Why do you tell people you're an accountant?"

"I thought everyone knew claiming to be an accountant was a cover for sex work." She laughed.

I felt so naive right now, so dumb. "It is?"

"I probably should have realized you wouldn't know that, considering your virgin status. How did that even happen? You're gorgeous. I'd have thought you'd have a line of men waiting to have you."

Heat rose in my cheeks. I wasn't embarrassed about the fact I'd never had a man touch me like that. Considering how I grew up and the bubble my parents put me in, it was astounding I'd even managed to move out on my own. They brought a whole new meaning to the word 'strict'. I was barely allowed to breathe without them on me. I felt so suffocated growing up and when I finally moved away I didn't know how to react to men.

Even my boss.

Mr. Black was a good man, but his hotness overwhelmed me. When I first started working for him twelve months ago, I found it hard to even talk to him. I'd gotten over that, especially as trust started to build between us, but it wasn't easy.

"I had ultra-religious parents," I said. "Remember? I didn't have any freedom growing up. I wasn't allowed to talk to boys and be around them alone."

Neither was Krissy, but she broke those rules all the time. I knew for a fact my twin sister was not a virgin. I also knew she lost her virginity at seventeen to Matthew Pinner, a jock asshole on the football team.

"Well, you're in luck," Kyra said, "because we definitely have openings for 'accountants.'" There was a hint of amusement in her voice before she turned serious again. "You need money?"

"Yes."

"How much?"

I winced. "The kind that comes with lots of zeroes." I peered down at the invoice. "Lots and lots of zeroes. I'm in the hole," I admitted. "I'm behind on everything and I'm getting desperate."

"You should have come to me." Krissy voice was soft and caring.

"I wanted to, but I was embarrassed."

"Honey, we're friends. You never have to be embarrassed."

I exhaled a deep breath. "I'm coming to you now."

"And I have the perfect solution for you and your money troubles. What are you doing Friday night?"

Considering I couldn't remember the last time I did anything other than work, I resisted the urge to laugh at her question. "Nothing. Why?"

"There's a virginity auction happening at the club."

Her words took a moment to sink in. "They auction someone's virginity?" My words were hushed, even though I was home alone. It felt weird, forbidden, to even speak them.

Kyra laughed. "You'd be surprised what men will pay for."

"You have got to be kidding."

"I'm as serious as your bills are."

I mulled it over for a moment. I was desperate. And what did my virginity matter if I couldn't keep a roof over my head, if I couldn't get my sister clean?

I blew out a breath and closed my eyes. I needed this. What choice was there? A minimum wage job waitressing or working in a bar? I'd still not make enough money to keep on top of my piling debt. It would be a one off anyway. It's not like I could become a virgin again after it was taken.

Could I do this? *Really* do it?

"Okay, tell me more," I said, before I changed my mind.

"It's simple. You'll be auctioned and

whoever buys you will get to take your virginity."

She made it sound so easy. I wasn't sure it was. My parents had always drilled into me the importance of waiting until I was married before I had sex. Letting a stranger pay to have my first time was a strange concept. I wasn't sure how I felt about it.

I glanced down at the invoice again.

What choice did I have? Maybe it was time to stop being the goodie two shoes everyone expected me to be. Where had that gotten me anyway? I'm deep in debt, drowning in it, actually. I was desperate. If I didn't do something soon I was going to lose everything, including my sister. I needed to find a way forward.

I channeled my inner Krissy.

What would she do?

She'd do the damn auction and she'd do it with her head raised.

I was tired of always doing the right thing. I needed to do the necessary thing.

I needed money and Kyra had a solution that would help. It was only my virginity. What did it matter who had it? What good was it to keep ahold of it when I couldn't afford to live my life?

"What is it like?" I asked.

"What?"

"Being a sex worker?"

"Liberating."

That one word made me feel at ease. My freedom was something I'd consistently strived to achieve after my overbearing parents. My sister might have seemed like a drain on me, but I owed her too. The small amount of freedom I'd had growing up was her doing. She'd pushed back against the rules and that enabled me to live a little more.

"I'm in charge of what I do there," my friend went on. "I don't push any boundaries I don't want to and the things I've tried are things I'd never do with a vanilla partner. Everything is safe. It's a reputable club, Jessica. I would never suggest this if I didn't trust the owners. They have an in depth vetting process for members. Each person has to be fully checked out. Any behavior that is deemed to go against the rules sees that person kicked out of the club. You'll be perfectly safe. You couldn't ask for a better environment to do this in."

That helped with some of the anxiety I was feeling. If Kyra thought it was safe and liked it there I trusted it was.

"How long have you been doing this?"

"A while now. Long enough to trust it's a good place to work."

"How much would I get?" Selling off my virginity had to be worth my while.

"Depends on the bidding, but it would be a lot of zeroes." Amusement laced her voice.

That statement made hope flare inside me. Could I really find a way to get ahead? To stop worrying about money? To breathe a little easier.

I decided to stop over-thinking and just do it. "Okay."

"We'll go shopping tomorrow to get you ready."

Ready? What did I need to do to sell my body? "Ready how?"

"You're going to need the right outfit."

I frowned. "What kind of outfit?"

"Leave that to me."

I huffed out a breath, a little relieved I had

her here to give me the information I needed, and to guide me along the way. The last thing I wanted was to make a fool of myself. "Is there anything else I need to do to get ready?"

"Maybe," she murmured as she contemplated what I'd need to do. "Maybe I should just come over. I'm guessing you've never had a Brazilian?"

I winced at her statement. "I'm a virgin. I've never had anyone."

"Oh, my sweet summer child," she said with a light bit of laughter. "You have no idea how much you need me right now."

"I'm home if you want to come over." I really did need her. I had no idea what I was doing.

"I'll be there soon." There was a pause, then. "Jessica?"

"Yeah?"

"I don't know what is going on with you or why you need so much money, but I'm here if you want to talk about it."

I did, but I was scared to open up, to show my sister in a bad light. I sighed. "Thank you. You're already doing everything I need by getting me into this auction."

"Love you, girl."

"Right back at you."

I hung up and tapped my phone against my chin, unable to believe I was really going to go through with this.

CHAPTER 4

Donovan

The club was the last place I wanted to be. I don't know why but a place that was once my sanctuary had started to feel like a noose around my neck. I didn't get the same enjoyment out of it that I once did. For someone with my sexual proclivities the club offered a range of activities. Somewhere a little out there. Somewhere kind of vanilla and uninteresting.

My need for something more exciting in the bedroom was why I had my own secret pleasure dungeon at home. It was why I came to the club too. I was constantly searching for something more. Something fulfilling.

I'd yet to find it with any of the women I'd been with.

I sipped my whiskey as I watched the room fill with people. The dark walls and low lighting made the club feel sexy yet with an edge to it. It was easy as a first timer here to feel overwhelmed and even a little scared, but I'd never known anyone have a bad experience in the club. It was set up to ensure everything was safe and consensual.

The themed nights at the club could be fun. Last month they had a whole evening dedicated to flogging. Virgin auctions were not my thing. I didn't get the fascination with virgins. I wanted a woman who knew what she liked in bed and how to give me what I liked too. I didn't want to spend the whole time fumbling through sex.

I wanted a woman who loved pain as much as pleasure.

I wanted a woman who I could tie up and play with.

Virgins didn't fall into that category.

I loved the club, but I don't know what the fuck they were thinking doing this. Truthfully, I wasn't sure what the fuck I was doing here either.

Archer convinced me to come, but I was considering making a break for it. The only thing that kept me standing by the bar was the fact that I was interested to see what kind of women would be involved in this kind of proposition.

I watched people moving through the room. Unlike usual, most of the women were wearing dresses. I'd never seen so many people in this room so covered. Usually, everyone was in various stages of undress. There was a woman wearing a dress that split along the middle to show her midriff. She caught my attention because of the silver belly chain shimmering as she walked past me.

I found myself wondering what that would look like on Jessica.

Especially if Jessica was naked and only wearing that chain.

I don't know where the fuck that thought came from, but it made me jolt. I should not be thinking of my pretty little assistant naked, with a belly chain wrapped around her narrow waist. I straightened my shirt, trying to focus my attention.

My eyes shifted to the make shift dais the club owners had erected in the middle of the room. It meant buyers could get a three hundred and sixty degree view of their purchase.

I leaned against the bar as Archer approached me wearing a suit similar to mine. "I'm glad you came," he said.

"What else was I going to do?" I muttered.

"Are you planning on bidding?" he asked.

"Fuck no. I'm only here because you twisted my arm."

Archer smirked. "You don't fancy yourself a hot little virgin?"

"Why would I want someone I have to break in?" I sipped my drink, relishing the burn as it slid down my throat.

"Because you can mold her to whatever you want. Don't write virgins off, Donovan. They have their perks."

"You sound like you're talking from experience."

"Maybe." His eyes twinkled as he smiled. "Maybe you should throw caution to the wind and bid. You might enjoy yourself."

"Auctions aren't my thing."

"Reserve judgment." Archer grinned as he spotted someone he knew through the crowd. "I'll be back. Try not to bankrupt yourself by bidding."

I snorted at his enthusiasm, but that was not happening.

The lights dimmed and a series of spotlights were focused on the stage area. I leaned back against the bar and tried not to let my irritation bleed through.

The owner of the club stepped onto the stage and explained how the auction would work. I half listened, knowing I wasn't going to bid. Cheers went up as he announced the first virgin.

Her name was Chelsea and she was twenty-four. I wasn't sure if that was her real name, but she was wearing next to nothing as she stepped on to the dais. She looked nervous, but kept her smile in place as the bidding got under way.

She seemed timid, not someone I would

usually pick. I was dominant in the bedroom, but I needed my submissive partner to be able to speak up if she was uncomfortable. I didn't want someone I could walk over. I needed someone strong to be my match.

I had no idea if this girl knew what she'd gotten herself into. The men in the club were vetted, handpicked by the owners, but that didn't mean they weren't animals in the bedroom. There was a reason they indulged their kinks in a sex club.

I didn't like to judge, but I knew the kind of men they were because I was one of them. I needed to be in control of my partner. I needed her to relinquish that to me.

The girl sold for just shy of fifty grand to one of the regular patrons. I don't follow the second sale, focusing on watching the first woman talking with her buyer. It wasn't my place to step in or say anything. She'd willingly done this, but I did wonder if she knew what she'd really gotten herself into.

I was so focused on that I didn't see the third woman that was brought out.

"How much will you pay for Jessica?" the

auctioneer announced. "Let's start the bidding at twenty thousand."

Something made my eyes shift back to the stage. The woman on it was younger than the other two had been. She was beautiful too. Her long hair tumbled down her back and her makeup was heavy but sexy. She was wearing a tiny pair of panties that barely covered her and a matching bra. Her figure was stunning, her skin looking like silk under the lights.

She was also familiar.

It took me a moment to realize who I was looking at.

Jessica.

My fucking assistant.

I wasn't sure which thought to focus on first—the fact that she was auctioning off her virginity in the sex club I frequented, or the realization that she was a virgin, or how hard my dick was looking at her practically naked body.

I've always been attracted to Jessica. From the moment she walked into my office, I couldn't keep my eyes off her. She was so damn innocent, and I was the kind of man who would destroy that innocence. She deserved someone who would love her and treat her gently. I could never do that. It wasn't in me to be that way in the bedroom.

Jessica's eyes skated around the room and I could see how nervous she was as the bidding got underway.

Some regulars were eying her like she was fresh meat, quickly placing bids. My stomach churned. They'd eat her alive. Jessica was beautiful and smart, and the thought of these fuckers taking her virginity made me want to roar like a caveman.

How the fuck could I leave her to these animals? One of them was into extreme punishment. Nipple clamps, flogging, orgasm denial. Jessica wasn't ready for that. She'd never even had sex—something I was trying desperately to wrap my head around. How did someone as beautiful as Jessica still have their virginity? And why the hell was she selling it?

I'd suspected something was going on with her, but if she'd needed money she could have asked me. I would have given it to her. I would have done anything to help her.

I lifted my hand, joining in on the bidding.

I shouldn't, but I couldn't let them have her. I wouldn't be able to live with myself if I let one of these men lay a finger on her.

I'd protect her innocence.

I'd keep her safe, even if it was from herself.

"Didn't think you were going to bid," Archer said as he sidled up to the bar next to me.

I didn't answer him. I kept my eyes locked on the stage.

I wasn't sure Jessica could see me past the lights shining in her face. She shifted anxiously on her feet and looked as if she desperately wanted to cover her body with her hands. I wished she would.

I'd thought about seeing her naked curves more times than I could count. It had filled endless fantasies I'd erected in the twelve months since she'd been at my company, but I never could have imagined the first time I'd see her it would be like this —on stage, selling herself to the highest bidder.

My hand went up again to make another bid.

The figure kept rising. Fifty grand, sixty, seventy. Money wasn't an object. I had plenty of it and I'd pay whatever it cost to keep her safe. The other bidder finally bowed out at a hundred thousand dollars and the bid was closed.

I should have felt elated at winning her, but my mouth pulled into a tight line as I moved to the stage. My anger was growing. Why the fuck did she do this?

As I stepped onto the stage to collect my prize, Jessica's eyes widened. I might have taken a moment to recognize her, but there was no confusion in her gaze. She knew it was me instantly.

I stared at her, uncertain whether I wanted to yell at her or cover her up. I opted for the latter.

Shrugging out of my suit jacket, I wrapped it around her shoulders. Her cheeks were flushed, even beneath the caked on makeup.

"Off the stage." I gave the order through gritted teeth.

When she didn't move immediately, I grasped her wrist and tugged her to get her moving. She wobbled on her heels and trailed after me as I dragged her into one of the private rooms off the main area.

As soon as the door was closed behind Jessica, I stared at her, not sure what the fuck I wanted to say, but needing to say so much.

In the end, I settled with, "Get dressed. I'll take you home."

"Are you pissed?" she asked in a voice that was bolder than it should have been considering the circumstances.

"Get dressed, Jessica. Now." We were going to talk about this, but in a sex club was not the place to do it. "I'll be outside. Don't keep me waiting."

It was going to take all of my control to keep my hands off her. I'd bought and paid for the privilege, but that didn't mean I could have her. She was still my assistant, she was still a helluva lot younger than me, and despite all those reasons I still wanted her more than I'd ever wanted anything.

CHAPTER 5

Jessica

Donovan was clearly not happy. After I got dressed, he led me out to the car and ordered me into the back of the vehicle. I pulled his jacket further around my shoulders as I watched him through the window as he spoke with his driver. I wondered what he was saying. I wasn't sure if he was really taking me home or if he was taking me somewhere to get what he'd bought and what was now his.

My virginity.

The thought of Donovan Black taking my virginity didn't suck. I'd been attracted to him since I started to work for him, but I got the impression he wasn't impressed by my actions tonight.

I wasn't ashamed of what I did. I needed the money and I leveraged what I had to get the cash, but the way he kept glaring at me made me wonder if I should have been embarrassed.

Had I gone too far?

You sold your virginity, Jessica, undoubtedly you went too far...

I was in a bind and I did what I had to, I reasoned. One hundred grand was a lot of money and it would see me right for a while —at least long enough to get ahead and make things comfortable for me and Krissy.

I glanced over at Donovan, who was now sitting beside me in the back of the car and focused on the side window as his driver eased onto the main road.

It was wrong of me to think it, but he looked handsome tonight, even in profile. He was wearing one of his tailored suits, the white shirt open at the neckline. It was fitted well, showing the outline of his pectorals. I wondered if I should offer him his jacket back, but I didn't want to give it up either. I liked how it smelled. It was infused with his cologne and a masculine scent that was all him.

"Are you going to say anything?" I asked after a moment. The silence was making me crazy.

"What is there to say?" he snapped, finally looking at me.

"I don't know," I said, finding myself bristling at his own attitude. "Why did you buy me?"

"You were in a den of vipers and completely unaware. I did what I needed to do to keep you safe."

That statement warmed me even as it annoyed me. I didn't need to be protected. I wasn't a damsel in distress. I was a grown ass adult who knew exactly what I was doing.

"I knew exactly what I was getting into," I argued. Kyra had been very thorough in briefing me about what to expect.

He growled a curse under his breath and my ears warmed at the dirty language. I'd seen Donovan Black at his best and at his worst over the past year. I'd never seen him this pissed though. He was fuming. I was surprised there wasn't steam coming out of his ears.

"The fact that you believe what you just said shows exactly how little you know about what those men in the club expect of you."

I fell silent, not sure what to say to calm the anger thrumming through him.

"I was safe," I said, lifting my chin stubbornly. "Kyra told me everyone in the club was vetted, that there was a process for becoming a member."

"There is, but that doesn't mean you were remotely safe," he said though his clenched jaw. "The men in that club would have eaten you fucking alive."

Why was he so angry anyway? Did I embarrass him? The company? I was his assistant. People would talk if they knew...

Shit, had I screwed things up at work?

I hadn't even considered that would be an issue.

Then again, I hadn't expected my boss to be at a well-known sex club...

"Am I fired?" I asked.

He made a grunting sound in the back of his throat. "No, you're not fired."

This made me frown. "Did I embarrass the company?"

"I don't give a fuck about the company right now," he snapped.

"Then why are you so furious?" I demanded, out of ideas. I'd never seen him like this, especially not toward me. He was acting as if I'd somehow betrayed his trust.

He turned his body more toward me, in a much more intimidating way. "Why do you think?"

"Honestly, I don't know."

"Because you were on the stage of a sex club wearing nothing but your goddamn underwear while men bartered over who was going to take your virginity. *That's* why I'm pissed, Jessica. You are better than that."

His words hit a chord, one I didn't like. It made me feel shame, like I'd done something wrong. I hadn't. My body was mine to do what I wanted to with it, even if that meant selling something viewed by society as important.

"What do you care if I sold my virginity?" I asked. "It's not like it matters."

"It fucking matters," he argued.

"Why?" I pushed him, wanting to know his reasoning.

"Because your first time should be with someone who will take care of you, who will show you how good it can be," he replied, his tone still gruff. "Do you think whichever bidder bought you would ensure that? Or even care about your first time being any good? They want a virgin because it fulfills some twisted fantasy in their head of being the only man inside your sweet pussy. Do you think they would be gentle with you?"

I didn't, but I didn't want to admit that either. I was still firm in my decision. It was the right one. The only one. I was up to my neck in debt. What other choice did I have?

"I needed the money," I blurted out. "I was out of options. Believe me I didn't want to do this either."

Donovan gritted his teeth. "There were plenty of other options. Talking to me for one."

His holier than thou attitude grated on

my nerves, which were already shot from the auction. If I was being honest I'd admit I was on edge the entire time I was standing on that stage being bid on. I had no idea who was trying to buy me. I hadn't been able to see past the glaring lights.

"You have money," I pointed out. "You'll never know what it's like to have bills piling up without a single idea of how you're going to pay them. You've never been so desperate that the only option to keep yourself afloat is to sell your body to the highest bidder."

I watched as he turned back to the window, his jaw tight. "No, I've never been in that position," he agreed, looking marginally calmer when he glanced at me again. "I can't imagine how it must feel to be drowning with no one to throw you a life preserver, but you didn't need to resort to this."

"What else could I have done?" I demand, my voice rising. "I needed a lot of money and fast."

"I understand you're clearly in trouble, but I'm a little hurt that you didn't come to me, Jessica. I could have helped. Instead, you resorted to selling yourself to a room full of predators."

"You were in that room too," I pointed out. "Are you a predator?"

His eyes snapped to mine, irritation flaring through them. "Of course not."

"But you're a regular there?"

"Clearly," he muttered.

That intrigued me more than it should have. Donovan had always been an imposing figure. He was smart, successful, handsome too, so knowing he was a member at a place like that baffled me. He could get any woman he desired.

"Why do you go to a sex club?" I asked, my curiosity getting the better of me.

"I know you're innocent, Jessica, but surely you're not that naive." The bite in his words had me sinking back into the leather.

"I'm not naive," I muttered. "I just want to know."

He shifted his shoulders. "Why does anyone go to a sex club?"

"To have sex?"

A small smirk flirted at the edges of his

mouth. "To have sex with certain... requirements."

I was innocent when it came to sex, but I had a vague idea of what a club might entail. A dungeon filled with toys and chains and leather paddles for spankings . . .

The thought made me rub my thighs together as my pussy clenched.

I wondered what that would feel like?

I wondered what it would feel like to have *him* do it to me—

I stopped that thought dead in its tracks. I did not need to be imagining my boss smacking my ass.

"You go there to meet women?" I asked instead.

The thought of him with others made my stomach churn. I didn't expect him to also be a virgin, but I didn't want to think about his past conquests either.

He sighed heavily. "Sometimes."

"Did you intend to buy someone tonight?" I persisted. "Was that why you were there? Were you looking for a virgin?"

"No. I have no interest in virgins, Jessica. The idea doesn't interest me."

I tried to ignore the sting of his words, but failed. Did that mean he didn't want me? "But you bought me," I pointed out.

"Yes."

"Why?"

"I already told you it was to protect you." He huffed out a breath. "Why didn't you come to me when you realized you needed so much money?"

I pushed my hair back from my face and huddled deeper into the warmth of his jacket. "It didn't seem prudent to beg for a fifty thousand dollar raise."

Assistants were not paid close to that—especially not one with as little experience as I had. This was my first job in the field and I was probably about to be fired.

I watched as he scrubbed a hand over his face as he digested the figure I gave him. "Can I ask what it's for?"

I winced because I was going to have to deflect this. I wasn't about to tell him about my tragic life and my issues with my sister. I wasn't ashamed of Krissy, but I didn't want his sympathy either. I didn't want him to look at me differently.

"I'd rather you didn't." My voice was low when I said it, my eyes going to my interlaced fingers in my lap.

"Okay." I thought he was going to leave it there and not press, but then he said, "Are you in trouble? Can you at least tell me that?"

"Not the type of trouble you're thinking," I said. "I don't have loan sharks or the mafia after me."

He didn't laugh. "How can I help?"

"Paying a hundred grand for my virginity is more than enough help," I said, trying to lighten the mood. It didn't help. His jaw got even tighter. "So… hotel? Penthouse? Where are we going?"

I said it lightly, but if I was being honest I was nervous. I was also glad it was Donovan who bought my virginity. Now that the reality was starting to sink in I was realizing it could have been a total stranger's car I was in the back of—not my insanely hot and pissed boss.

"How'd you know about the penthouse?" he asked.

There wasn't any heat in the question, but a middling curiosity. Considering how involved I was in his personal and professional life he should have known. "The contract you needed me to bring over to have signed that holiday weekend... it was for a penthouse apartment."

"Right." He paused and I wondered what he was thinking. "How about I just take you home?"

For some reason his words stung. It was ludicrous, ridiculous even, to feel upset about the fact that he didn't want to sleep with me, but I did. He had bought and paid for me. He should have wanted to collect what he was owed.

Why didn't he?

Was I really that repulsive?

Did he not find me attractive?

Did he not even want my virginity?

If I was going to give myself to anyone I was glad it was him, but that feeling was evidently not mutual.

I was disappointed. All the fantasies I'd had about him, I'd convinced myself they would just remain that way—as fantasies—because a man like Donovan Black could never be interested in someone like me.

Apparently that voice in my head was right, because he wasn't.

"Oh. Okay. Sure," I said quietly. "Whatever you want to do."

I gave the window my attention, unable to look at him.

I felt shame slither through me, far worse than the shame I felt at selling my body to the highest bidder.

"Jessica." He said my name softly, but I didn't turn to him. I didn't want him to see that I was fighting back my tears.

"It's fine. I probably should go home. It's been a long day."

The car turned the corner a little sharply and I scrambled to grip the seat, but it was no good. I slid into him and he grabbed my hips to steady me.

My eyes lifted to meet his, my heart thudding in my chest. I feel electricity zap through my body at his touch. I needed it. I craved it and I craved him. This was never going to be enough for me. I wanted to be more than employer and employee.

I wanted Donovan and I was going to do whatever it took to have him.

CHAPTER 6

Donovan

As I held her against me to keep her from sliding off the seat, my heart gave a solid thud in my chest. Fuck, but I wanted her. The way her eyes met mine made my body take notice. She was beautiful and for better or for worse I was the owner of her virginity.

Part of me, the possessive side, wanted to take her. I could see the disappointment shining in her eyes when I suggested taking her home. She didn't want that. She wanted something different. She wanted me. Jessica wasn't good at hiding her feelings. She wore all her emotions on her face, which made it easy to read her.

It also made it hard to say no to her.

I'd paid for her. I'd bought the right to take her.

It still didn't feel right.

I'd bought her to protect her from others who would not be kind to her.

Fucking her would change everything, and not necessarily for the better. We would always have this between us. I wasn't keen on being someone's first, though I would admit, the thought of being the only man inside Jessica did make me want to beat my chest like some kind of primal caveman.

It was a stupid fucking reaction, but it swirled around my thoughts, planting seeds of ideas. I wanted to be her first.

I wanted to show her the kind of pleasure she'd never imagined existed.

I didn't want to ruin the way things were between us, though. There was a lot that could go wrong when relationships were changed like this.

What if things went sour?

What if she couldn't stand being around me and she quit her job?

I couldn't lose her—not like that.

Not at all, if I was being honest with myself. I'd come to rely on her in my life, both personal and professional. I didn't want to upset the status quo.

Her fingers gripped my biceps, bringing me back to our current situation. She was holding on to me, like I was a life raft keeping her afloat. Her lashes fluttered before she peered up at me. I don't know why the fuck she was wearing all that makeup. She didn't need it.

I wanted to be inside her.

Instead, I dipped my head. Our mouths were inches apart, and I was sure she was holding her breath because I had no illusions that I was holding mine.

"Have you ever been kissed, Jessica?" I asked, wondering how innocent she was. Was it just her virginity she had to lose? Had she done other intimate things with men?

"Not much," she admitted, her cheeks flushing pink.

It made me smile until I realized I was not the kind of man who she needed. She couldn't deal with someone who demanded what I did in the bedroom. I couldn't corrupt her.

"You're far too innocent for someone like me," I said, scanning her face, as if memorizing every inch of it. I committed her image to my memory banks because I had no idea how much tonight would change things between us.

"I'm not as innocent as you think," she said, her voice a little husky, as if she was fighting to keep herself under control.

I certainly was. I was fighting the overwhelming urge to push her back on the seat and dive between her legs. I wanted to swirl my tongue around her sweet pussy and eat her up until she moaned my name.

"I don't believe you," I said. She screamed innocence and it wasn't an act. She was completely naive.

"Maybe," Jessica admitted, and briefly bit her bottom lip. "But maybe that just means I need you all the more."

"This is a big step," I said, meaning it. "You shouldn't just give your virginity to anyone."

Her eyes were big as they took me in and I could see the desire in them. I was sure I was reflecting my own back. "I *want* it to be you."

"Why?"

"Because I trust you."

Those words floored me. I tucked a piece of hair behind her ear, needing to touch her in some way, no matter how small. I needed to connect with her and to feel connected to her. "You've waited this long, Jessica. Surely you can wait a little longer for a guy to come along that you love."

I wanted her to say no, that she couldn't wait, even though that was selfish of me. She should have someone who would love her. Not someone like me. I would want to dominate her.

"Actually . . . I've waited a long time for you," she said, surprising me.

"What?"

"I've wanted you for the past year. You've always been it for me. I thought that could never happen, that you were out of my reach and off limits, but now... now, we have a chance."

I wasn't sure what to do with this information. I had no idea she'd liked me all this time. I thought back, trying to discern if there were any signs of her feelings. She was always quick to help me, going over and above what any other assistant had ever done. I thought it was because she was keen to prove herself. Now, I was wondering if there was a different reason entirely.

Telling me how she felt about me was like putting a flame to oil. Emotions burned through me, ones I wanted to explore. Because if I was being honest too, I'd admit I've desired her, as well. The only thing that stopped me from crossing lines that couldn't be uncrossed was the fact that she was my employee.

But clearly I leapt over that line tonight when I bought and paid for her virginity. There was no going back. We were different people compared to the start of the night. Our relationship was forever changed.

"Jessica..." I whispered her name, afraid to

say it. "I'm too old for you. I'm your boss. This isn't right."

Even as I said the words I wanted to take them back. What did I care about age differences? What did I care about her being my employee? I'd never kept to the rules, but then I'd never crossed business with pleasure either. I kept my sexual proclivities separate from my professional life.

No one, apart from Archer and possibly Jessica's friend Kyra, knew I went to the club. No one was aware of the things I liked to do in that club. I didn't think Jessica would be able to handle all I would want to do to her. She'd never look at me the same way. I would terrify her.

But the thought of having her beneath me while I pushed into her slick heat was thrilling.

I craved that.

And the more I thought about it the more I *needed* it.

She gripped my hands in hers, her eyes filled with promise and hope that I didn't want to dash.

"What if I've been waiting for this sexy

older man to notice me?" She breathed the words, her eyes never leaving mine.

Fuck, I had a lot of self-control but she was pushing me past the point I could withstand. How was I supposed to fight this?

"Is that what you've been doing?" I asked.

Jessica glanced down at our joined hands. "It's not a big deal." She was wrong. It was a huge deal. "You never noticed me like that anyway."

I released her hands and hooked a finger under her chin. "I noticed you. Believe me, I noticed."

Another rush of heat rose in her cheeks, turning them a beautiful shade of pink. "You did?"

"I'm not blind," I told her. "You're stunning, but whether I want you or not isn't the issue here. You should wait to be with someone you love. Your first time should be special."

"Was yours?"

"No it wasn't and I regretted that for a long time."

"What if this is my only chance with you?"

"Jessica…" I breathed her name.

She might be innocent, but I wondered if she knew what she was doing to me right now. I wondered if she realized the sway she had over me, the ability to break me down completely.

Sitting this close to her and not kissing her was fucking torture. I wanted to claim her mouth, *claim her.* I wanted to fix her problems and make her smile again.

It was taking all my resolve not to take something that should never have been on the table for me in the first place.

"I'll hate myself for blowing this opportunity if I let it pass by," she said.

Fuck, she was making this so hard. I was only human. There was only so much I could take before I cracked.

"You may hate me for going through with it," I said, but I couldn't resist reaching out and brushing my knuckles over her cheek. She leaned into my touch, ready to take whatever I was going to offer her.

The best thing, the sensible thing, to do was take her home, let her pay whatever she owed with the money she'd received at the auction, and return to normal. But I didn't think there was any chance we could ever return to who we were before tonight. She could never just be my assistant again, and I could never just be her boss.

I was the man who paid for her virginity.

And she wanted to give it to me.

That surprised me more than anything.

"I could never hate you," she whispered. "Please, Donovan."

It was the first time she'd ever used my name. She was a stickler for calling me Mr. Black when we were in the office. I understood why. She wanted to show respect, but hearing my name on her tongue unlocked something in my chest. It made all my resolve flee. How was I supposed to resist her when she was begging me for this?

I didn't think. I didn't contemplate the downsides or the trouble it could cause.

I leaned forward and I pressed my mouth to hers.

I wanted to give her soft and gentle, but I didn't have it in me to do that. Instead, my kiss was possessive and hard. I crashed my lips against hers, letting her know I owned her in this moment. I would take her virginity. I would give her the best night I could, making her first time special, because I was a bastard.

A better man would have walked away.

I couldn't.

I wasn't that strong.

I didn't have that much willpower.

I scraped my fingers through her hair, getting a handful so I could turn her head the direction I needed to deepen the kiss.

Wanting her to open up, I teased my tongue along the slit of her lips, begging entry. It took her a moment to realize what I was doing, but as soon as she did her mouth opened and I thrust my tongue against hers.

She was tentative with her movements, but she wasn't shy. She wanted this as much as I did and that spurred me on. I wanted to take her here and now, in the back of the car, but I wanted time with her too. I needed to have her spread out on my bed while I ate her pussy.

I wanted to play with her, but she wasn't ready for that. Not yet. Maybe in time I could introduce her to my pleasure dungeon.

She made a little whimpering sound that

went straight to my cock. There was no chance in hell I could refuse what she was offering. I wasn't that strong.

I pulled back from her kiss and spoke to the driver, asking him to take us to the penthouse, rather than Jessica's apartment.

I returned my attention to her, my mouth suddenly dry as I scanned her face. She seemed pleased with my decision so I pressed my mouth to hers again.

We made out until the car idled at the curb outside the building. She climbed out first and I followed, slipping my hand into hers.

Crossing the foyer and passing the concierge, I walked her to the elevator and stabbed the button to call it. She didn't say a word as we waited for it come and I wondered if she was having second thoughts. We stepped into the elevator when it arrived. What was she thinking?

She hadn't let go of my hand, so I took that as a good sign.

When the elevator doors opened on the penthouse floor, I turned to her. Fuck, she was gorgeous.

"Are you sure?" I asked, giving her the chance to back out.

It would kill me to let her go, but I'd put her back in the elevator and have my driver take her home if she said the word. I knew I was a lot to take in the bedroom. I also knew once I started this there was no way in hell I'd be able to stop. I wasn't sure an innocent young woman like Jessica could handle everything I wanted to do to her.

I wasn't sure she'd be able to take my pleasure dungeon.

Jessica raised her eyes and gave me a smile that made me want to push her against the wall and capture her mouth.

"I'm positive."

CHAPTER 7

Jessica

As soon as Donovan opened the penthouse door, he pulled me inside and pressed me against it. He ground his cock against my core, making sparks of pleasure roll through me. I couldn't stop the whimper that tore out of my mouth. I'd never been touched like that and it ignited something inside, a deep carnal need I didn't know I possessed.

His mouth latched onto mine, his tongue sliding past my lips. I was grinding against him as he pressed me harder against the door. I didn't have the first clue what I was doing, but I ached fiercely between my legs and rubbing against him was the only way I could soothe it.

His fingers cupped my breast as he continued to kiss me as if I was his oxygen. His movements were hard and unyielding. I wanted everything he was offering and more. I just didn't know what that was.

That thought made a little tendril of anxiety slither through me. What if I wasn't good. What if I did it wrong? Was there a wrong way to do it?

Was it going to hurt?

Nervous energy made me pull my mouth from his, needing a moment to breathe.

He let me go, his eyes scanning my face. "Are you okay?" he asked.

"Yeah."

He stepped away from me. "Why don't we have a drink? Slow things down a little?"

I wasn't sure if I was happy about that—did we need to slow things down at all?—but I nodded. He rolled the sleeves of his shirt up, exposing thick forearms. I stared at them before I slid my eyes up to watch as he moved to a narrow cabinet. He pulled out a bottle of dark amber colored liquid.

"Scotch okay?"

"Sure," I said, even though I'd never drank it before. He already thought I was stupidly naive. I didn't want to give him the impression that extended to other areas of my life.

I sat down on the couch, taking a moment to look around.

The suite was impressive. There were huge windows spanning the full length of two walls that looked out over the city. We were high up and the view was incredible. The horizon was filled with lights, twinkling in a way that chased the dark sky above away. It was late, but it was clear the city was still largely awake.

The room was filled with masculine style furniture. A square sectional in gray and a large flat screen on the wall opposite it. There was a dining table too, which made me wonder how often he entertained here—if at all. He didn't seem the type for elaborate dinner parties.

As he stepped in front of me, I brought

my attention back to him. He held a tumbler out to me with a little less than two fingers worth of alcohol in the bottom of it.

I wrapped my fingers around the glass, liking how my skin scraped across his as I did.

He took a sip of his own as he moved over to the entertainment center near the television. I watched as he opened a cupboard filled with vinyl records.

"I didn't know they still made vinyl's," I said.

"It's the only way to listen to music," he murmured as he scanned the shelf.

I raised my glass to my lips and took a long swig. It scorched my throat as it went down and as it hit my stomach it felt as if it warmed me from the inside out. It was strong, malty, and I wasn't sure I liked the taste, but I took another gulp of it anyway. I liked how it made my limbs feel looser the more I drank. I wasn't a huge drinker, though my drink of choice was something more cocktail based. The scotch was stronger. A lot stronger.

"What sort of music do you like?" I asked,

placing my empty glass on the coffee table in front of me. I was still wearing his suit jacket, but it was warm in here—or at least I felt warm—so I slipped it off.

"Anything and everything. My tastes range from rock to classical."

He pulled a record from the sleeve and put it on the turntable.

It started to play. I didn't recognize the song, but the background noise was welcomed. He turned back to me and the heat in his gaze made me squirm. He was looking at me like he wanted to devour me— and I wanted him to.

"I'm sorry," I said nervously.

He sipped his drink, savoring it. I should have clearly done the same. "For what?"

"I don't know how to act."

"Just be yourself."

"I'm not… sexy."

He'd bought my virginity. Did he expect me to give him a show too? I wasn't the kind of girl who could dance and flirt. I didn't know how to do either.

"On the contrary," he said, sliding his glass on the cabinet so he could grab the bottle.

He walked over to me and poured another measure in the bottom of my tumbler. I was grateful for that. I already felt looser with the alcohol floating through my veins.

His eyes locked to mine as he recapped the bottle. "I find you to be sexier because you're not trying. So… be yourself, especially with me."

Be myself… right.

I took a big gulp of the scotch, once again relishing the burn as it slid down my throat, then I set my glass on the table. The song changed and this one I knew—not well enough to sing along, but well enough to sway to it.

I got to my feet, feeling more at ease, and started to move in time to the music. I let myself go, found my rhythm and twisted my body with it.

I felt Donovan behind me and his arm came around my waist, pulling me against him. I could feel his cock pressed against my ass as he held me firm. His nose went to the crook of my neck, making me tilt my head to give him better access to that sensitive area.

His hand gravitated south, almost touching over my pussy, which throbbed with need.

His fingers cupped me between my legs through my dress, his palm grinding against me. I whimpered as he swayed behind me, moving us to his rhythm. His movements were fluid and easy, which seemed like a good sign. Kyra would say so anyway.

I found myself grinning at that thought, but everything scattered from my thoughts as he kissed my neck.

"I want you," he told me in a deep, husky tone of voice.

I shivered, my nipples puckering into tight points. "I want you, too."

He took his hand from between my legs and scooped me into his arms. I let out a small squeak of surprise as he settled me against his chest, my arms hooking around his neck. Donovan carried me into the bedroom. I barely had a chance to take in the furnishings before he laid me down on the mattress.

He was so gentle, so caring. I didn't antic-ipate that. I wasn't sure how I expected this night to go, but it wasn't in my boss's bedroom. I never thought I'd get to have Donovan. My fantasies were becoming reality and I wasn't sure if I wanted to wake up from this dream.

As soon as I was laid on the bed, Donovan stepped back and rubbed his thumb over his bottom lip as he examined me. "Fuck," he muttered, appreciation in his voice.

It made me flush. He saw me in a way I didn't see myself.

When he didn't move and just kept staring at me, I felt a little uncertain. "What is it?"

"You're gorgeous."

I didn't think I was unattractive, but my parents were not fast and free with compliments about my appearance. I always felt different from other women my age because no one had ever touched me. My parents made it impossible for me to meet someone growing up, but since I left home and struck out on my own I still hadn't taken that step.

I didn't know why until this moment.

I was waiting for him.

For Donovan.

I needed him to be my first; I just didn't realize it.

He would make it good for me, I knew that, but how would I make it for him? I didn't know how to have sex. I didn't know how to pleasure him. I didn't know how to do anything. What if I was lousy at this? What if he hated every moment of our time together?

Performance anxiety washed through me, making me pull my lip between my teeth.

His eyes focused in on it immediately. "You're biting your lip. Are you scared?"

I wasn't scared of what he was going to do to me. I knew he would treat me well. I'd known Donovan for a year. I knew he was a decent man.

I was more nervous he would be disappointed in me.

He'd paid one hundred grand for this night. Even if he'd done it to protect me originally, I still felt like it was a lot of hype to live up to.

"I'm afraid," I admitted.

He tilted his head to the side, considering me. "Of what?"

"That I won't be good enough."

It made me cringe to admit it, but my fear was real. He didn't mock me for it. Instead, he shook his head, as if he was annoyed by my own doubts.

"That thought should never have crossed your mind," he said. "We'll take it slow. If you want to stop at any point just say the word."

That assurance eased some of the tension in me, even knowing I wouldn't want to stop.

Slowly, he leaned forward and pulled me up until I was standing in front of him. Then, he lowered the zipper on my dress and let it fall to the floor at my feet. It shouldn't have been hot, but him undressing me the way he was made my pussy wetter than it already was.

My panties followed a moment later. He guided them off my feet, dropping them on the floor before he took my shoes off. I felt exposed without my panties and just my bra on, but he didn't let me keep that for long. He reached behind me and unfastened the hooks, his fingers scraping over my back.

He freed my breasts and I instinctively tried to cover my nakedness.

"Don't," he said, his voice husky. "Don't hide from me."

He pulled my hands gently away as he cupped my breast. His thumb caressed over my nipple, making it pebble. I was sure I might expire as pleasure shot between my nipple and pussy. It was as if the two were connected.

I arched my body as I threw my head back, moaning. It didn't sound like me. I'd never heard that noise come out of my mouth, but I liked hearing it.

Donovan dipped his head down and kissed me as he guided me back on to the bed. When he straightened, he started to undress himself. I watched as he unbuttoned his shirt. It felt like I'd waited a lifetime for this moment and I enjoyed every moment of it. He shrugged it off his shoulders revealing his muscled chest. He wasn't overly built, but it was clear his gym sessions had paid off.

His pants went next. I was enthralled as he freed his cock. It was thick and veiny and I was wondering how the hell it was going to fit inside me. He didn't seem to have that concern. Donovan gave it a tug before he moved back to me.

He hooked his hands under my thighs and pulled me to the edge of the bed, so my ass was overhanging the edge slightly. I planted my feet firmly on the floor, my fingers gripping the sheets as he went between my legs.

The first touch of his tongue to my center nearly made me jolt off the mattress.

I sucked in a breath and held it as he swirled his tongue around that sensitive nub that made my body twitch with need. He was talented—not that I had anything to compare it to—but I'd never felt this way when I'd gotten myself off before.

It was as if he knew exactly where to touch to make me writhe on the bed. I was gripping the sheets so tight I was sure I was going to leave half-moon nail marks in my palms.

I felt my orgasm growing, my pussy contracting as the waves started to wash through me. I was going to come. My breath was ripping out of me as I climbed higher and higher with each flick of his tongue.

Then it hit me.

It was like an explosion going through my body. I cried out in pleasure and tried not to squeeze my thighs together, but it was hard not to.

He stood while I had the most amazing sensations rippling through me.

I heard him move to the bedside table and open it. There was a rustling sound before he came back to stand in front of me. When I looked up I saw he was wearing a condom.

"Up," he ordered.

I did as I was told, scrambling off the bed. He laid down in my place and I frowned at him.

"I want you to lead this, for you to have control."

I smiled at his words. "How do we…"

"Climb on top of me." I did as he asked, straddling his hips.

He guided his cock into my hand and gently pressed it between my folds. "Gravity will do all the work," he told me.

I wasn't sure what I was doing, but I slowly lowered myself onto his cock. It slid through my wetness, pressing at my entrance. Sex was supposed to hurt, so I was a little hesitant to push further. Donovan rubbed my thighs, reassuring me.

I pushed further onto him, feeling my pussy stretching around his girth. It burned and I winced as I waited for my body to adjust to his size. I felt weirdly full of him, and I wanted him deeper inside me.

I braced my hands on his chest as I slid lower on him. It felt like I hit resistance, as if I couldn't go any deeper, but I didn't think he was that deep inside me.

"Jessica," he spoke softly, bringing my eyes to his. "You're okay."

I was. I pushed through the barrier. Pain flared through me, deep inside me. I cried out, gasping as I froze. He kept stroking my thighs, the motion soothing.

I needed to move.

I pulled back slightly. It hurt a little. I pushed back onto him and the burn started to morph into something else. I felt full, that aching in my pussy changing into pleasure. I used my hands to move up and down on him, pushing him deeper inside me with each stroke. He watched me, his hooded eyes never leaving mine. He started to move his hips, pushing his cock even deeper inside me. I gasped and moaned with each stroke as we set a steady rhythm.

I could feel my climax building again. I arched my back as I ground down and exploded around him. My pussy contracted, and with a deep, guttural growl he released his own orgasm. His hips faltered, his rhythm interrupted as he came. I pulled free of him, whimpering at the loss of him inside me. He pulled me into his arms, gathering me next to him, and kissed my head.

I didn't know it could be this good, and now that I'd had him I wasn't sure I wanted to give him up.

Donovan

I didn't want to wake up. My body felt used and tired. I'd fucked my pretty little assistant well last night and I'd made sure she had a good first experience—and second and third—so when I opened my eyes I was surprised to find the bed next to me empty. I ran a hand over the sheets, which were cool.

I climbed out of bed, letting my feet scrunch in the carpet before pushing up. I'd envisaged sinking into Jessica's pussy more times than I could count over the past few months. She wore those tight-fitted pencil skirts that hugged her curves and heels that made her calves look amazing. I never thought I would be able to have her—not like this.

Taking her virginity was a dick move, but I was glad it was me and not someone else. I knew the men who frequented the club. They wouldn't have gone easy on her. Her first time would have been traumatic. I hoped I made it good for her.

I headed into the bathroom and leaned into the shower cubicle to turn the spray on. The water came down, the room filling with steam. I tested it before stepping under it.

She'd looked so beautiful last night. She'd ridden me, her breasts bouncing as she slid up and down my shaft. That image would be engraved in my brain. If nothing else ever happened between us, I'd never forget that view.

I'd never forget how it felt to slide inside her slick channel and have her push through the barrier of her virginity.

I leaned a hand against the tiles. I needed

to find release before my balls exploded. I was riled up, ready to go for round four, but I guessed Jessica might be a bit sore after what we did and I wasn't that much of an asshole that I'd put my own needs before hers.

Instead, I reached down. Palming my throbbing cock, I slowly pulled up and then down. My balls instantly reacted to the touch, tightening. I continued to jerk myself off. As I did, I kept her image in my mind.

I imagined it was her sliding up and down my shaft, rather than my hand. I imagined grabbing her tits as I fucked her tight cunt. My hand moved faster, twisting slightly as I did. My legs started to feel weak. I locked my knees in place as I increased my strokes.

My breath started to tear out of me and my balls were even more strangled as I kept going. When my climax tore out of me the force of it nearly drove me to my knees as streams of cum spurted from the head of my shaft. I groaned and slowed my hand action as I milked my cock dry.

Breathing hard, I leaned my head against the tiles while waiting for my pounding heart to slow. Jessica was under my skin and I wasn't sure I wanted to get her out from under there.

I closed my eyes and wondered where the hell we went from here. I wanted her to remain as my assistant, so I'd do whatever was needed to ensure she felt comfortable at work, but this changed the dynamic between us and I was going to do everything in my power to make sure Jessica was *mine*. I wasn't going to let her go without a fight.

I tilted my head under the shower head, letting it wet my hair completely. I scrubbed my body and scalp, then I washed myself off.

Once I was done, I turned the water off and stepped out. Grabbing a towel off the rail, I wrapped it around my hips and went back into the bedroom.

I dried and pulled on a pair of sweatpants. There was still no sign of Jessica. I was starting to consider she might have had regrets about what we did and left this morning.

I didn't think she was the kind of person who would run away without talking to me, but we'd never been in this situation before.

Plus, I was learning she wasn't always

forthcoming with me. She'd lied for however long about her money troubles. Jessica wasn't quite the open book I thought she was.

Now that I'd tasted her, I wasn't going to let her go or walk away. If she thought she could push me away she was wrong about that, too. I was in this now. I felt like I wanted to claim her in every way that mattered, and it was a powerful emotion.

I'd never experienced this kind of thing before.

I fucked women. I didn't want to settled down with them. But I definitely wanted that with Jessica. Except, I didn't know if she would accept me if she knew the truth behind the suits and expensive cars—if she knew about my pleasure dungeon and all the depraved things I wanted to do to her in it.

I left the bedroom and made my way into the living area. The TV was on low, but there was no sign of Jessica. I frowned and grabbed the remote control, hitting the power button to off.

Moving through the penthouse, I searched for her, but she was nowhere to be found.

Then I saw the door was open to my pleasure room.

My stomach twisted. I didn't lock it. I never had reason to. If I brought a woman back here she knew my tastes, my proclivities already. Jessica was the exception.

She wasn't aware of my dominant side that craved her submission, or the sadist in me that enjoyed inflicting pleasurable pain, before she came here. I wasn't sure she was ready to find out about it either.

Not yet. We could have built up to this introduction, but my sexual preferences were a lot to take in for someone as innocent as Jessica was.

I walked up the hallway toward the door, my heart starting to race. When I stepped through the door, I wasn't sure what to expect, so it took me a millisecond to realize Jessica was sitting on the bed.

It wasn't an ordinary bed. There was a cage underneath the mattress and there were hoops on each bedpost. Ropes could be threaded through those rings. The sheets were silk and black, the walls were painted dark too. There were various pieces of equipment around the room that were able to hold a partner still while I did things to them. There was a cabinet filled with sex toys too. Butt plugs, vibrators, dildos. Everything imaginable that could bring pleasure or pain.

She didn't look up at me as I cleared my throat.

"I was worried where you went," I said, feeling the wall she was erecting between us already starting to grow. She looked wide eyed, and a little scared of what she was seeing.

"You shouldn't be in here," I added in a soft voice.

"I know. I'm sorry," she said. "I wasn't snooping. I was looking for the restroom."

It didn't enter my head that she'd been snooping at all. "It's okay, Jessica."

She hugged her knees to her chest as she continued to sit on the bed. She still hadn't looked at me and I wondered what was going through her head.

Finally, she asked, "What is this room?"

I wasn't sure how to answer that question, not without opening her up to a whole new world she wasn't ready to experience. And there was also the fear of her opinion of me changing, that she'd see me as a sexual deviant, and not in a good way.

I wanted to sit with her, but I stayed standing, not wanting to freak her out even more. "It's… difficult to explain."

She finally gave me her eyes and I didn't like the upset look on her face. "Try. Please."

Her gaze shifted to the x-shaped cross in the corner. It had padded manacles hanging from the top and bottom that were used to secure someone to. I'd had a lot of good times with that device and various play partners.

An image of Jessica with her arms stretched over her head and her legs spread out made my cock twitch in my sweatpants. Now was not an appropriate time to get a hard on, but she brought that out in me. She made me want things I didn't know I could have with her.

"I have certain… needs." It was one way of putting it.

"What kind of needs?" she pressed when I stopped there.

I exhaled a deep breath and opted for flat-out honesty. "I like to dominate my partners. I like to play with them."

Jessica's eyes grew a bit wider as she glanced around the room once again. "Is that what this room is? A room for playing sexual games?"

"Yes. I know things might look . . . scary, but everything in here is designed to bring pleasure, Jessica."

She lifted her chin in the direction of the rack containing various floggers and canes. My eyes followed her line of sight. "Even those?"

A small smile touched my mouth. "You'd be surprised how good it can feel. There's something about having your control taken from you, of having someone mix pleasure with pain, which releases all sorts of pleasurable endorphins."

"You'd *spank* me with those things?" she asked incredulously.

Fuck. I would gladly pull her pants down right now and redden her ass if she asked for it. She wasn't going to though. Jessica looked like she was barely keeping her shit together.

"If you consented to it, yes. Everything

that happens in this room is done with permission and a high level of trust." I let her take that in.

She narrowed her gaze at me. "Why would I consent to you hurting me?"

"It's not about causing pain, Jessica, or deliberately causing you harm. I know from the outside looking in it can seem like an imbalance, like abuse even, but it's neither of those things. I can only do to a partner what she allows. If something is off the table, it's called a hard limit and I respect that. I would never do anything that wasn't agreed to. It's a mutual understanding between two parties. The person receiving the punishment has to be comfortable."

"How can being smacked with a cane be comfortable?" Her voice rose in pitch.

"It's hard to explain," I said, shoving my hand through my hair.

"Please *try* because I'm struggling here, Donovan."

So, I did. "There's a thin line between pleasure and pain, but as a dominant I'd never give a woman anything she couldn't handle mentally, emotionally, or physically.

And that pain . . . well, it has a way of morphing into what is called subspace, which is the ultimate peak of pleasure."

I risked moving to sit next to her. She didn't pull away or run, which I took as a good sign. She was teetering on the edge right now and I needed to be careful not to push her over it. I knew this room was a lot to take in. I was a lot, too. She'd only ever viewed me as her boss. Now, she was glimpsing behind the veil that kept my true desires hidden.

I swallowed hard, nervous energy moving through me. This could be the end of this thing between us before it even had a chance to begin. I didn't want that to happen. I wanted to build on what we'd started, but that choice was out of my hands and sat firmly in Jessica's.

She might never want to see me again after this. Hell, she might leave her job too, and the thought caused a pang in my chest.

She studied me for a long moment before speaking what was on her mind. "Did you not tell me about this room and your because you didn't trust me?"

"No. I trust you," I admitted, realizing it was true as soon as I said the words.

"But you kept this a secret."

"It's not the kind of thing you share with someone so . . . innocent," I said.

I watched as she pulled her bottom lip between her teeth, mulling my words over. "Did you think I wouldn't be able to handle the truth?"

Considering how scared she looked, I didn't think that was a bad assumption to make. "Jessica, this isn't exactly the kind of thing that is brought up in casual conversation."

She tipped her chin up. "So you didn't trust me or you didn't think I could handle hearing you're a man with darker sexual urges?"

"Neither." She stared at me with her brow slightly cocked and I went the honest route again. "Both."

"That's what I thought."

She pushed up from the bed, unfurling her legs and I felt my heart rate pick up. Was she walking out? Was she done with me? Did

I fuck this up before it even had a chance to get started?

"Jessica—"

"I've worked for you for a year. A full year," she hissed at me, and I was taken aback by the vehemence in her words. "I thought that would have earned a modicum of your trust. That you would have told me about all . . . *this*, before taking my virginity."

My lips flattened into a thin line of frustration. "It's not that simple."

"It is, Donovan. It's exactly that simple. You either trust me or you don't. You either think I'm not some naive little girl or you don't."

She went to the door and everything in me screamed to go after her. I didn't. I stayed rooted in my spot, watching the devastation play across her face.

"Goodbye, Donovan," she said.

Then she left and I felt something I'd never felt before. Devastated.

Her leaving gutted me.

CHAPTER 9

Jessica

$\mathcal{I}$ dressed in record speed and gathered up my stuff. Donovan didn't try to stop me or even come to see me, which I was grateful for. I didn't want to talk about what I'd seen in that room.

I knew there were people who were into… different things sexually, but finding out my straight-laced boss had a sex dungeon in his home, filled with all sorts of wicked, depraved items, threw me for a loop. And considering the elaborate set-up he had, it was clear that this lifestyle wasn't something he'd just stepped into. He'd been this way for a while.

Was he really into pain?

He had a lot of implements, toys, and devices in that room that could never be used to cause anything but discomfort, and if I was being honest I'd admit I was confused and freaked the hell out because it had been so unexpected and made me see Donovan in a whole different light.

Grabbing my purse, I shoved my feet into my shoes and rushed to the door. I glanced back in the direction of the room, a brief flicker of doubt making me wonder if I should go and talk to him, but I was scared by what I'd seen.

That room was like a torture chamber.

There was even a cage under the bed. Who had something like that?

As soon as I stepped out into the corridor, my heart started to pound harder. Would he try to stop me from leaving? I knew a big secret about a powerful man. Would he hurt me to keep it quiet?

I dismissed that thought instantly.

Donovan was many things but he would never hurt me. He'd been so kind, so gentle last night. He could have just taken what he wanted, but he didn't. The room and the man I knew just didn't match up. How could someone so good, so nice, be into spanking and delivering pain?

I stabbed the button for the elevator and when it didn't immediately appear I stabbed it again.

What the hell did I step into?

I wasn't sure if I was more upset I knew about his private room or more upset he'd never confided in me. Then again if this was the reaction he expected from me it was little wonder he kept it quiet.

As I calmed down, I realized I could have handled things a little better, but what was I supposed to do with all that information overload? The elevator arrived and I stepped inside quickly, hitting the button for the lobby.

I didn't relax until the doors shut. Then I sunk back against the wall of the elevator.

How was I supposed to go back to work on Monday? Did I even have a job anymore?

The money I earned selling my virginity would pay for Krissy's care and her stint in rehab, but after that I would have almost forty thousand left. It was enough to act as a buffer while I looked for new employment. I would be okay for a while and that stopped me from freaking out completely.

As soon as I stepped out of the penthouse building, I sucked in the fresh air. It had been a crazy night and I was ready to get home.

Hailing a cab, I climbed in the back and told him my address.

While it navigated through the early morning traffic, my phone rang. I expected it to be Donovan, but it wasn't. It was Kyra. I noticed a list of missed calls from her and winced. I hadn't even paid any attention to my cell once I'd left the club the evening before.

I swiped my finger over the screen and answered the call.

"Hey," I said.

"Where've you been?" Kyra demanded. "I've been calling you and you didn't answer. I was worried."

I winced. I should have at least told her I

was leaving with Donovan. "Sorry. I didn't think."

"It's okay, but where are you?" she asked, her tone more concerned. "Are you all right?"

Was I all right? I wasn't sure. "I don't know," I admitted.

"What happened last night?"

"Well… Donovan got what he paid for." I winced at how that sounded.

Kyra made an excited little squeal in the back of her throat. "And? How was it?"

"It was amazing." I couldn't deny that part of the night had been out of this world. "He made sure it was good for me."

"I'm glad it was Donovan Black who won you," Kyra said. "I knew he'd treat you well."

"It was good, until I discovered he's some kind of deviant," I muttered.

"Whoa, what are you talking about? He has one of the cleanest reputations at the club."

I wasn't sure how to explain what I'd seen, but I knew Kyra wasn't going to judge me if I stuttered and stumbled over my words.

"It's… complicated."

"How? Jessica, talk to me."

I winced and glanced in the direction of the driver, lowering my voice. "Well, he has a torture room."

"A what?"

"A torture room," I repeated. "I found it when I was looking for the restroom."

"Torture? Or pleasure?"

He'd said there was a fine line between both. Was there? Kyra seemed to be implying the same thing.

"I don't know. He had weird instruments in there, and devices designed to—" I glanced up again at the driver, who was focused on the road and not on me. Even so my cheeks heated as I said, "—cause pain."

Kyra sighed down the line. "Like what?"

"Floggers. Canes. Places to tie someone up. Lots and lots of toys. You know... *those* kinds of toys." Heat rose in my cheeks again. I was going to die of embarrassment before I got back to my apartment.

"Honey, did you even give him a chance to show you what that room is for?"

"No. I freaked and got the hell out of there."

"That's a shame. There's a lot of fun to be

had in that kind of room, Jessica. Someone like Donovan, with his experience, would be able to take you to the brink only to bring you back over and over. I'm a little jealous."

My mouth gaped open. "You are?"

She laughed. "Yeah, honey. I wish I knew a good looking businessman with a sex dungeon."

Okay, maybe I'd been a little rash. "I was scared and I thought the worst," I admitted.

"Okay, I'm coming over," Kyra insisted. "We need to talk."

"Thanks," I said and hung up.

When the cab pulled up outside my apartment, I paid the driver and headed inside. As I stepped inside my apartment, I felt claustrophobic, like the space was too small. I'd broadened my horizons last night in ways I didn't anticipate and although I didn't expect to feel differently, I did. I wasn't the same person I was when I left for the club.

And not because I was no longer a virgin, but because I'd crossed a line by fucking Donovan, *my boss*. It was a line that couldn't be uncrossed and I'd have to live with those consequences. The thought of leaving my job made me want to cry. I loved working for him and I loved spending time with him too.

I felt something more for him now that we'd had sex, and I had a feeling I'd done irreparable damage to any chance of us having a relationship by my snap judgment of his secret room and his sexual desires when I really hadn't given him the opportunity to *show me* that part of his life. I'd unfairly judged him based on my own fears.

I went into the kitchen and put on a pot of coffee, setting up the machine as my mind whirled. After I put it on to percolate, I grabbed two mugs ready for Kyra arriving.

She didn't take long to get there.

The pot had barely finished doing its thing when there was a knock on the door.

I opened it and was greeted with my best friend standing there. She gave me a look that was somewhere between sympathetic and annoyed before she pulled me in for a hug.

I went willingly, needing comfort. My head was a jumbled mess and I wasn't sure she could help put things into perspective.

"You okay?" she asked.

I nodded and then pulled back. "I'm feeling like maybe I panicked and overreacted." And in the process, I'd probably made Donovan feel like shit, which I hated.

Kyra closed the door and we made our way into the kitchen. I grabbed the coffee pot and made up our drinks while she took a seat at the breakfast bar.

"So, tell me everything from start to finish."

I did. I gave her all the details. Every last one. When I was done, she stared at me. "I'm going to tell you what all those toys and devices are for and what they do."

She pulled out her phone and typed something in before turning the phone back to me. "The cross you saw in the room is called an X-cross. It's designed to strap someone to it in a spread eagle position."

"Why?"

"Well, that's up to the couple to decide. I've used it many times. Sometimes a scene partner will use vibrators or dildos on me while I'm chained up. I can't move and that heightens the situation. There's something liberating about letting go and allowing someone else to take control."

I could see the appeal. Donovan had given me full control last night and it had made me feel powerful.

She pulled up another image. "These are nipple clamps. You put them on your nipples and the pain they cause is out of this world. I orgasm so hard every time I use them."

An odd heat flared in my stomach. "But aren't they uncomfortable?"

"Yeah, that's kind of the point though. They make all the blood rush to the tips and when you take them off..." she closed her eyes as if she was locked in a memory. "Best feeling ever."

I bit my bottom lip. "Okay so what about the cage?"

She shrugged. "Some people like to be degraded. It turns them on. The cage can be used for whatever the couple deems. For sleeping in, for punishment. Everything that happens in these situations is completely consensual, Jessica. You can only be pushed as far as you allow. Safety of the person having these things done to them is imperative. There's always a safe word that's used in case you want to stop."

"I shouldn't have run off," I groaned, covering my face with my hands. "I feel so stupid."

Kyra pried my hands away so that she was looking into my eyes. "You're not stupid. You're just innocent. The product of a sheltered, religious home can't be faulted for not knowing what sex toys are. I don't blame you and I don't think Donovan would fault you, either. He's a good guy. No one has ever said an unkind word about him." She chuckled. "Guys like him don't get turned down that often. You probably bruised his ego."

I winced. "He's never going to talk to me again."

"You don't know that. Go to him and explain. He'll understand. You're inexperienced, honey. He'll know this would have been a shock to you. I'm also a little jealous you have this stunningly handsome man who wants to pleasure you on demand." She smirked. "I would touch him all day if he'd let me."

That hit me wrong. I didn't want Kyra

touching him. I didn't want any other woman to touch him, either, for that matter. I wanted him to be all mine.

"It's never too late to make amends, you know," she said, oblivious of my possessive thoughts.

"How do you know that?"

"Because you're both still breathing." She laughed. "Go to him. Explain why you freaked. And I have just the apology idea you need. It will make him beg you to stay forever, and ever, and . . ." she let the words trail off as she giggled with excitement.

I didn't know what she had in mind, but I had a feeling it involved something new and a little bit scary. After what had happened last night, something new and a bit scary was okay with me. I hoped.

CHAPTER 10

Donovan

Jessica leaving the way she had was swirling around my brain in the hours afterward. Maybe I should have insisted she stay and talked to her, explained to her the kind of things I was into, but how the fuck did you have that conversation with someone who'd never even had sex before?

How did I tell her I liked spanking women and then getting them off until they were writhing with need?

She was naive and innocent in a lot of ways when it came to sex, and I'd scared the hell out of her. I could see it in her eyes before she ran out on me.

I was debating calling her when I heard a knock on the door. It was odd. People generally didn't knock on my door without the doorman buzzing up to tell me who was here. I wondered if it was one of my neighbors as I made my way to open it, but I never spoke to anyone in the building if I could avoid it.

I opened the door and stopped breathing.

It was Jessica. *My* Jessica.

She looked amazing. The heavy makeup she'd worn last night was gone and was replaced with more natural tones. Her hair was straight and framed her face beautifully. I took in the overcoat and black boots she was wearing, but it was her smile that drew me in.

I blew out a breath. "I wasn't sure I'd see you again."

"I wasn't sure either," she admitted, almost shyly.

I stepped back so she could enter and then I shut the door behind her.

I could tell she was a little nervous as I turned back to her. "I was out of line earlier," she said.

"No, you weren't," I said. "It was a lot to take in. I never meant for you to find that room without me explaining things first. I promise you, I don't go around hurting women."

"I know that," she said, and finally smiled. "Kyra explained it to me. About the room, about what goes on in there."

I was grateful to Kyra for doing that. It would have been better coming from her. Jessica would have been more likely to trust an impartial view, especially one from Kyra who was close to her.

"Right." I exhaled a deep breath. "What did she tell you?"

"That it's for delivering orgasms. Lots and lots of orgasms."

She removed her coat, letting it drop to the floor. My breath caught in my throat. She was wearing the most beautiful bra and panties I'd ever seen. Dark green lace that fit her perfectly and stockings that showed a slither of skin above the lace.

Fuck, my cock went solid instantly.

"I want you to show me," she said.

I scanned her face, hope rising within me. I was ready to give her the full tour, but she needed to be handled with care. This wasn't something I could rush. Baby steps before we moved onto the more intense games.

"You're sure?" I asked, holding my breath as I waited for her answer.

"Quite sure. Because I trust you."

My heart soared, and taking her hand, I led her through the penthouse and to the room. I could feel her trembling a little so I turned to her and pressed my mouth to hers. I didn't want her scared. I wanted her to enjoy every moment inside this space. I wanted her to plead to come back here time and time again.

Her lips were soft and the kiss was tentative at first before she found her boldness. I slipped my hand between us and cupped her pussy. Her panties were damp, which make me smirk.

"Is all this wetness for me?"

She whimpered as I rubbed her clit through the material. "Yes."

I liked that and I wanted to keep her wet. I took her over to the bed and ordered her to sit on the edge of it. She did as I asked, like a good girl. I liked that, too.

I opened the drawer at the side of the bed and pulled out a silk scarf.

"I'm going to blindfold you. Then you're going to lie on the bed and hold your arms over your head. You're not allowed to move unless I tell you. And if at any point you want to stop what's happening, you just need to say the word red."

She nodded her agreement, so I wrapped the scarf around her eyes, tying it at the back.

As I'd ordered, she lay back across the middle of the bed. I tugged her to the edge, so I could drop between her legs and pulled her panties off. "Don't move your arms," I told her, in a more demanding tone.

She held them high above her head and I couldn't help but think she looked beautiful spread out like this.

I took a moment to admire her before I

went to the toy cupboard and pulled out a bullet vibrator.

It was small but powerful.

It would make her scream.

I also grabbed a set of nipple clamps. I needed to be careful not to put them on too tight this first time. We could build up to more.

When I returned to the bed, I pulled her nipples into hard buds and attached the clamp to each one. She moaned a little as they pinched her nipples.

Then I ran my fingers through her folds, dipping one inside her pussy. She squirmed but kept her arms in place.

I switched the bullet on, the buzzing sound loud. Then I pressed it against her clit. Her hips twitched as soon as I made contact. I kept it in place, swirling it around that little bud, watching carefully to see which position made her pant the most.

Fuck, I could get used to this. I felt a sense of possessiveness come over me as I watched her writhe and whimper. So damn beautiful, and all *mine*.

"I'm going to..." she gasped and then her

thighs clamped together as her orgasm swept through her.

I watched her go over the edge, my cock solid as a rock.

While she was still in the throes of her orgasm, I dropped my pants and freed my dick. I grabbed a condom and rolled it over the tip before I gave my shaft a couple of pulls, making sure I was good to go. Then I lined up with her slit. I pushed inside and although I wanted to go hard and fast, I was aware she might be sore after last night, so I picked a slower rhythm. While I was fucking her, I reached up to pull the chain between the nipple clamps, which made her groan.

"Oh fuck," she gasped, and I felt her internal muscles clamp tight around my shaft.

My girl had sensitive nipples. That was perfect. It would mean we could have a lot of fun with nipple play.

I fucked her until sweat sheened on both of our skin. At some point she forgot about holding her hands over her head and was gripping my biceps. I'd let her have this lapse —next time I'd be sure to tie her down so she couldn't move. Or have a little fun punishing her for the infraction.

She went over the edge first, her legs twitching as her pussy squeezed around my cock. My balls tightened and I spilled inside the condom.

For a moment we both breathed heavily, trying to catch our breath. She pulled the blindfold down and met my eyes. There was heat and hunger in them and her face was flushed. "Will it always be like this with you?"

I wasn't sure what she meant by that but I leaned down and kissed her. "I'll always make sure you have a good time in this room," I said.

She smiled, relaxed and content and sated. "I can live with that."

I could, too. And everything else we'd figure out along the way.

SUBSCRIBE to my newsletter to receive a **FREE BOOK** not available anywhere else!

Don't miss the rest of the stories in the
Auction Series!

Follow KAYLEE MONROE on the Internet:
Kaylee Monroe Newsletter Sign-up
Kaylee Monroe BookBub
Kaylee Monroe Amazon Author Page
Kaylee Monroe Facebook Author Page
Kaylee Monroe Instagram
Kaylee Monroe Goodreads

www.ingramcontent.com/pod-product-compliance
Lightning Source LLC
Chambersburg PA
CBHW072053150726
47999CB00005B/1753